Evan Early

Written by
Rebecca Hogue Wojahn

Illustrations by
Ned Gannon

Woodbine House   2006

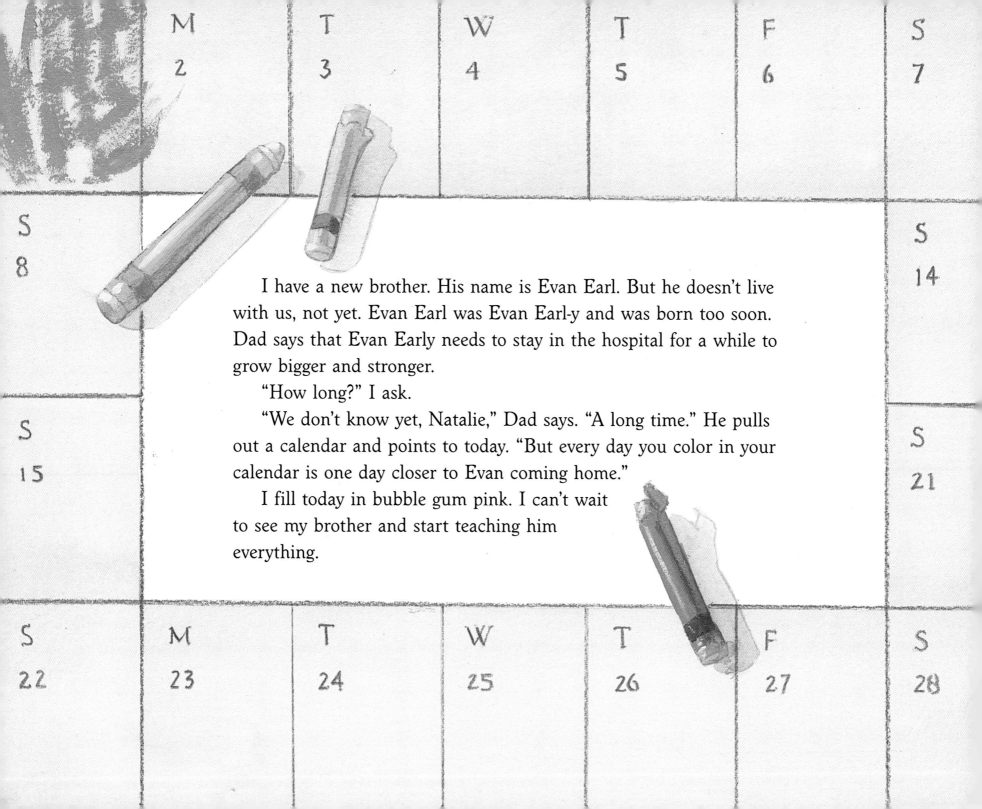

	M	T	W	T	F	S
	2	3	4	5	6	7

S						S
8						14

I have a new brother. His name is Evan Earl. But he doesn't live with us, not yet. Evan Earl was Evan Earl-y and was born too soon. Dad says that Evan Early needs to stay in the hospital for a while to grow bigger and stronger.

"How long?" I ask.

"We don't know yet, Natalie," Dad says. "A long time." He pulls out a calendar and points to today. "But every day you color in your calendar is one day closer to Evan coming home."

I fill today in bubble gum pink. I can't wait to see my brother and start teaching him everything.

S						S
15						21

S	M	T	W	T	F	S
22	23	24	25	26	27	28

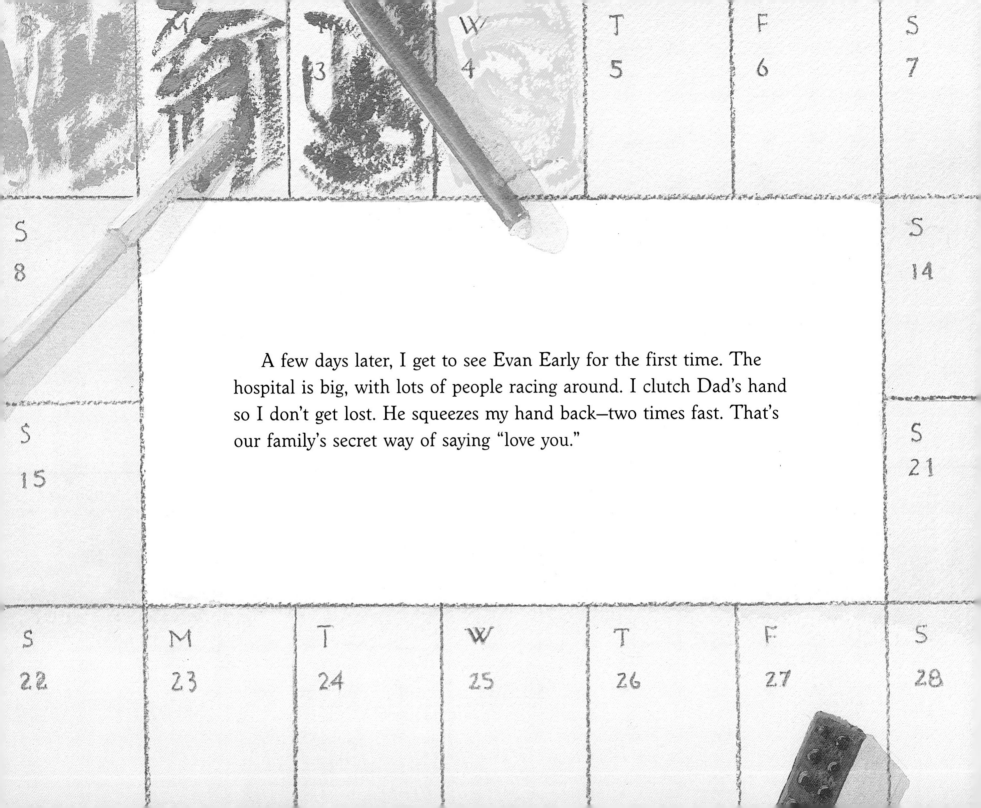

A few days later, I get to see Evan Early for the first time. The hospital is big, with lots of people racing around. I clutch Dad's hand so I don't get lost. He squeezes my hand back—two times fast. That's our family's secret way of saying "love you."

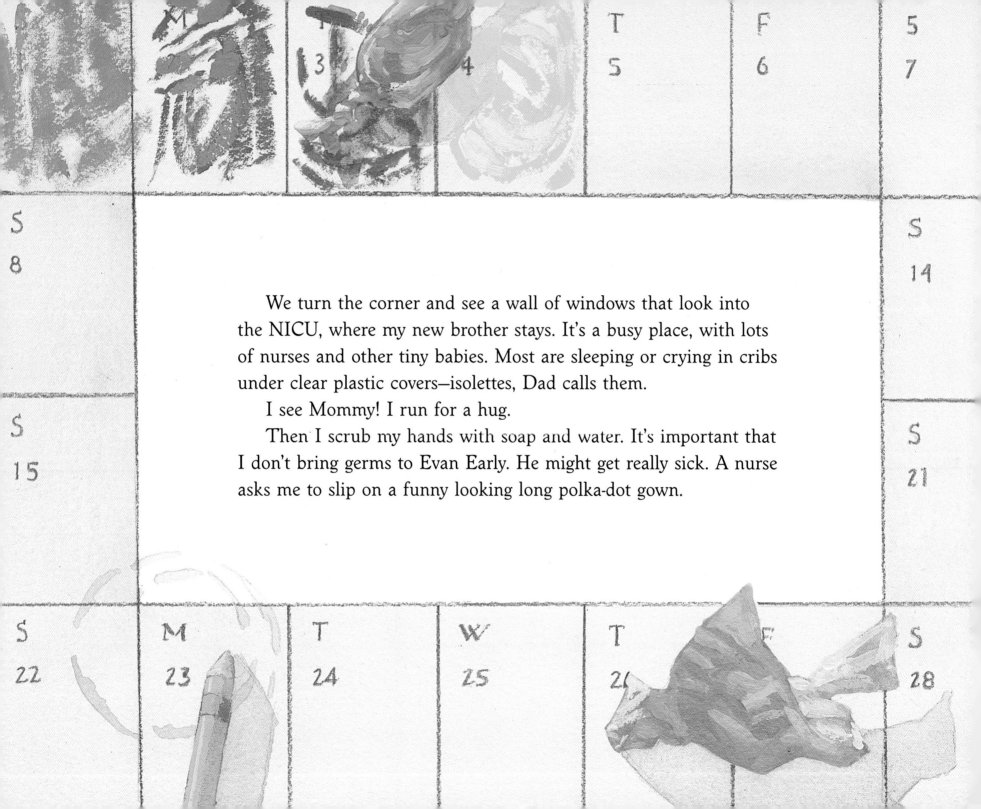

We turn the corner and see a wall of windows that look into the NICU, where my new brother stays. It's a busy place, with lots of nurses and other tiny babies. Most are sleeping or crying in cribs under clear plastic covers—isolettes, Dad calls them.

I see Mommy! I run for a hug.

Then I scrub my hands with soap and water. It's important that I don't bring germs to Evan Early. He might get really sick. A nurse asks me to slip on a funny looking long polka-dot gown.

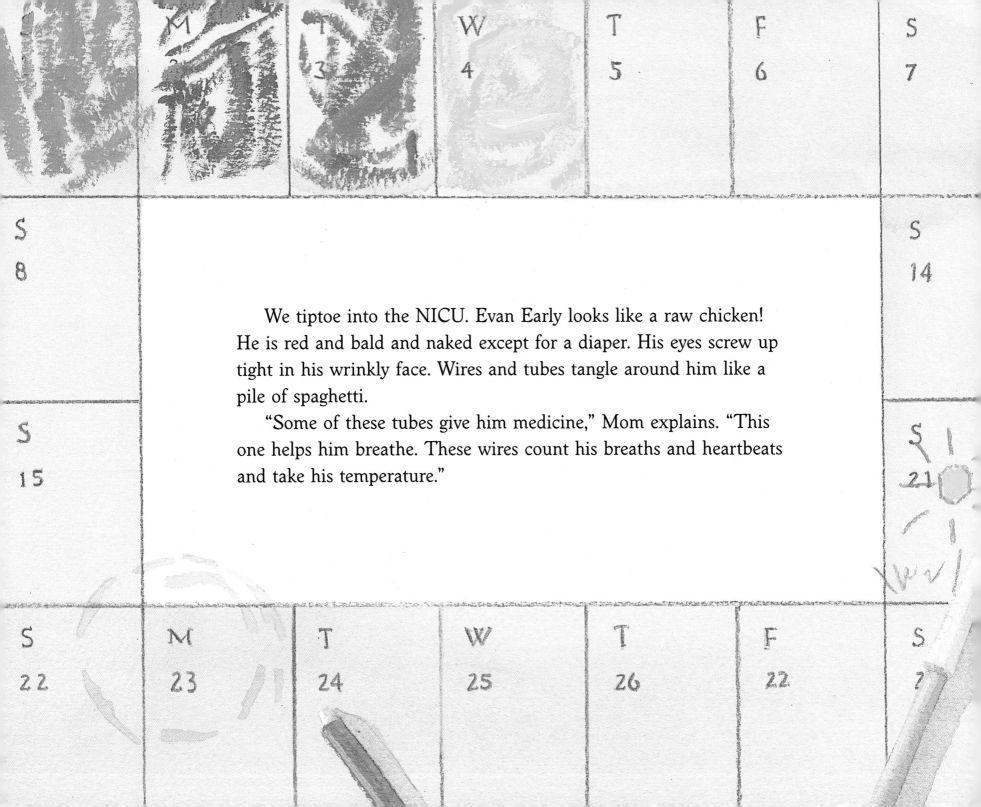

	M	T	W	T	F	S
	2	3	4	5	6	7

S						S
8						14

S						S
15						21

We tiptoe into the NICU. Evan Early looks like a raw chicken! He is red and bald and naked except for a diaper. His eyes screw up tight in his wrinkly face. Wires and tubes tangle around him like a pile of spaghetti.

"Some of these tubes give him medicine," Mom explains. "This one helps him breathe. These wires count his breaths and heartbeats and take his temperature."

S	M	T	W	T	F	S
22	23	24	25	26	22	2

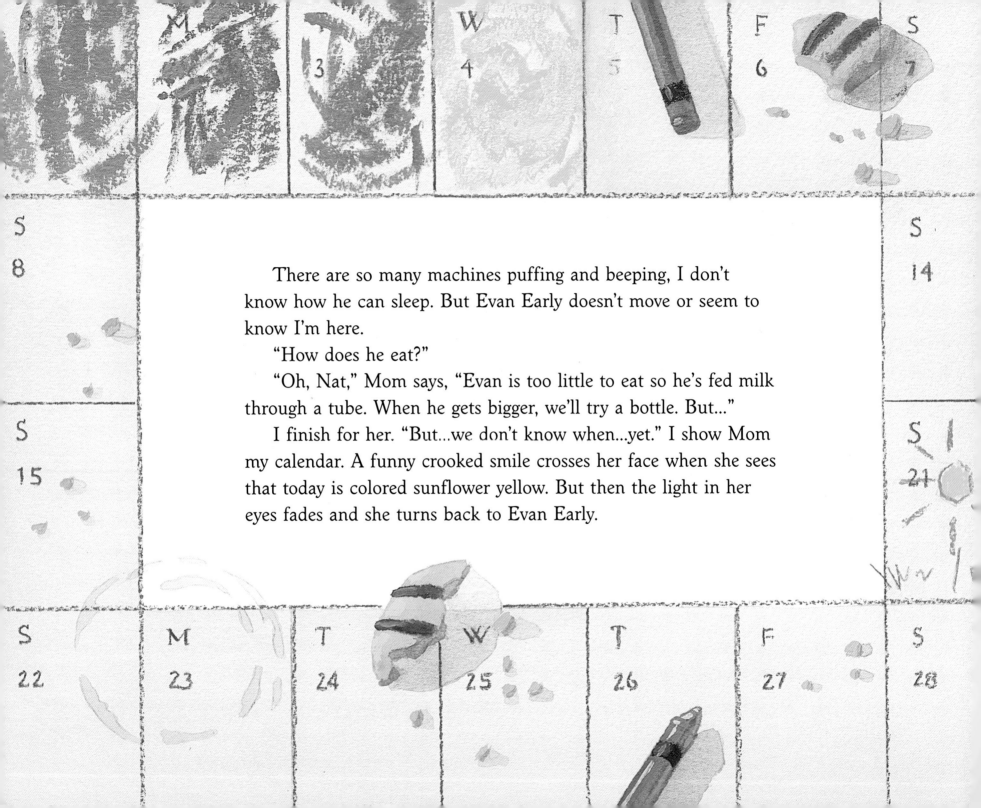

There are so many machines puffing and beeping, I don't know how he can sleep. But Evan Early doesn't move or seem to know I'm here.

"How does he eat?"

"Oh, Nat," Mom says, "Evan is too little to eat so he's fed milk through a tube. When he gets bigger, we'll try a bottle. But..."

I finish for her. "But...we don't know when...yet." I show Mom my calendar. A funny crooked smile crosses her face when she sees that today is colored sunflower yellow. But then the light in her eyes fades and she turns back to Evan Early.

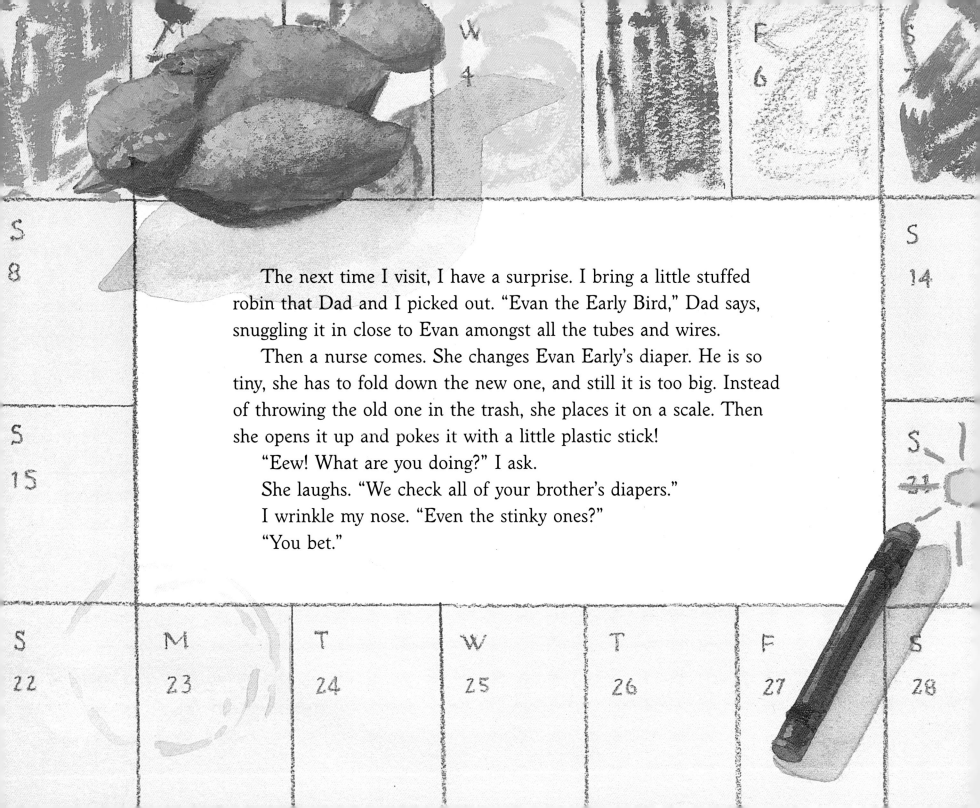

The next time I visit, I have a surprise. I bring a little stuffed robin that Dad and I picked out. "Evan the Early Bird," Dad says, snuggling it in close to Evan amongst all the tubes and wires.

Then a nurse comes. She changes Evan Early's diaper. He is so tiny, she has to fold down the new one, and still it is too big. Instead of throwing the old one in the trash, she places it on a scale. Then she opens it up and pokes it with a little plastic stick!

"Eew! What are you doing?" I ask.

She laughs. "We check all of your brother's diapers."

I wrinkle my nose. "Even the stinky ones?"

"You bet."

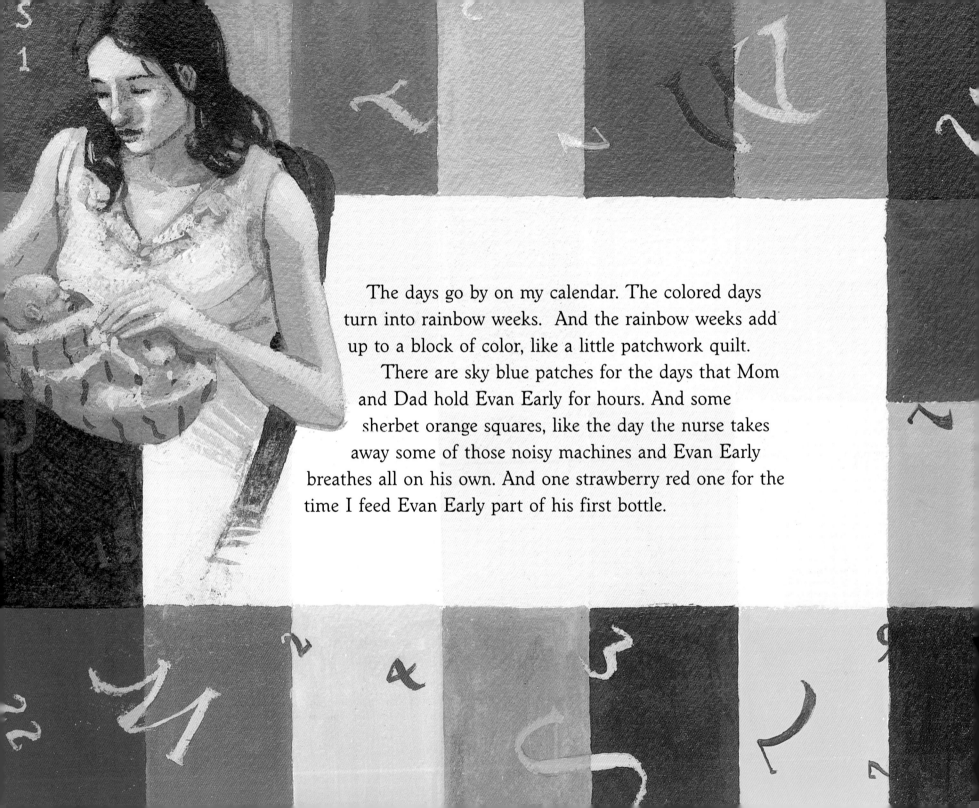

The days go by on my calendar. The colored days
turn into rainbow weeks. And the rainbow weeks add
up to a block of color, like a little patchwork quilt.
There are sky blue patches for the days that Mom
and Dad hold Evan Early for hours. And some
sherbet orange squares, like the day the nurse takes
away some of those noisy machines and Evan Early
breathes all on his own. And one strawberry red one for the
time I feed Evan Early part of his first bottle.

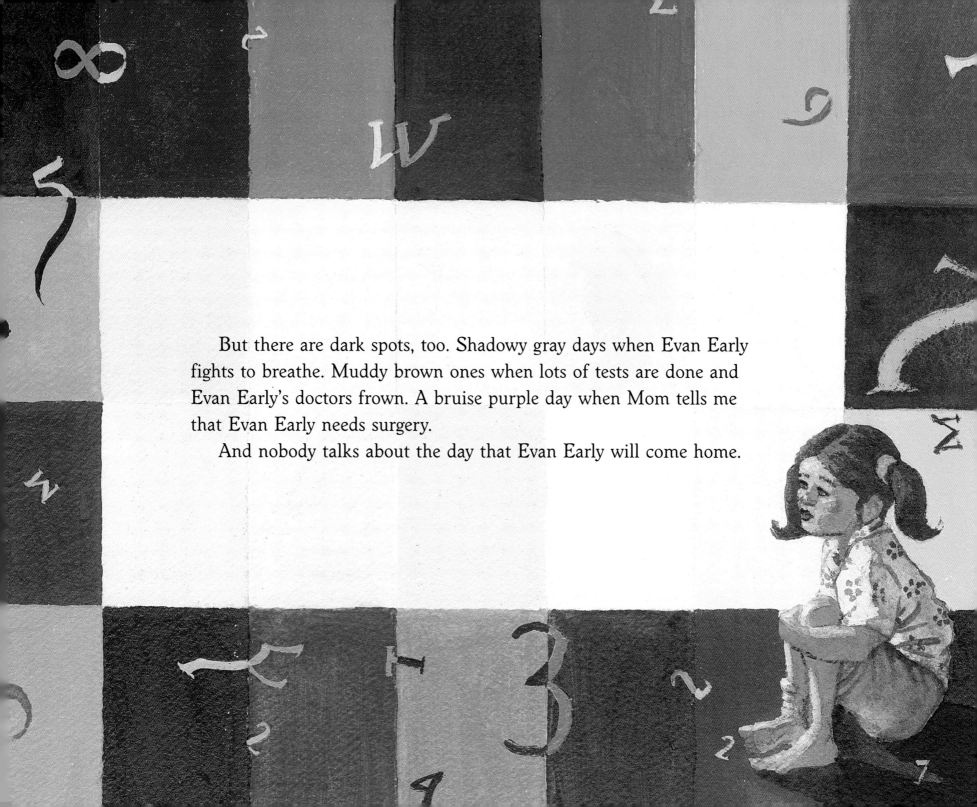

But there are dark spots, too. Shadowy gray days when Evan Early fights to breathe. Muddy brown ones when lots of tests are done and Evan Early's doctors frown. A bruise purple day when Mom tells me that Evan Early needs surgery.

And nobody talks about the day that Evan Early will come home.

Then—a monster black day. When Dad and I get to the hospital, doctors and nurses rush around Evan Early. They push me out. Mom leans on Dad, and Dad's mouth draws up tight. They don't even look at me, don't see the picture I've drawn Evan Early. Don't notice when Grandma comes to pick me up and take me home.

M
23

T
24

W
25

T
26

F
27

S
28

For two days, Dad and Mom stay away. I'm scared and lonely. Will Evan Early be okay? What if Mom and Dad forget about me?

At home I poke at my toys and flip through my books. Grandma makes a lot of quiet phone calls and lets me watch TV all day. She teaches me some new games, but they don't keep us from thinking about Evan Early.

Finally, Mom stumbles in the door on the third day. Her hair is flat. She wears the same clothes she did the last time I saw her. "Evan is getting better," she whispers as she hugs me. "His medicines are helping him grow bigger and stronger."

I take Mom's hand and pull her towards the game Grandma and I were playing. "Mom, let me show you. Do you want to play too?" I start setting up the game again.

Mom puts her hand on my head and says, "Not right now, Natalie."

"The park? Do you want to go? Or you could read to me." I grab a book.

Mom sinks into a chair. "Honey, I just need a shower. And maybe a minute to rest."

I throw my book across the room. "I'm getting bigger and stronger, too!" I shout. Then I run past her to my bedroom and slam the door behind me.

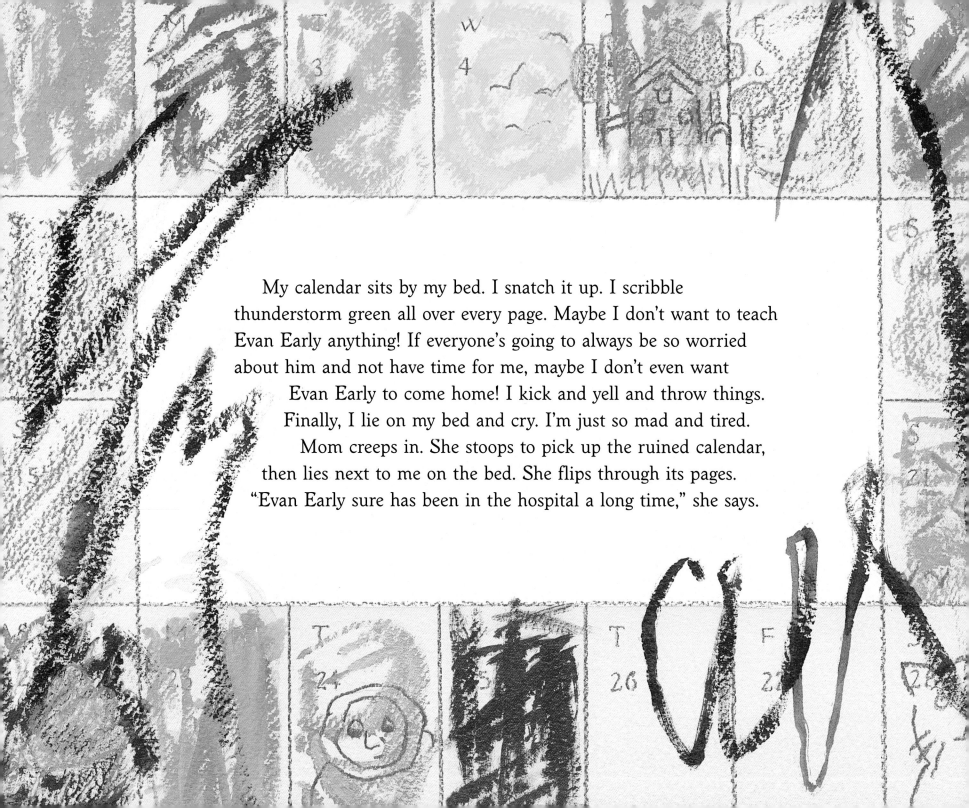

My calendar sits by my bed. I snatch it up. I scribble
thunderstorm green all over every page. Maybe I don't want to teach
Evan Early anything! If everyone's going to always be so worried
about him and not have time for me, maybe I don't even want
Evan Early to come home! I kick and yell and throw things.
Finally, I lie on my bed and cry. I'm just so mad and tired.
Mom creeps in. She stoops to pick up the ruined calendar,
then lies next to me on the bed. She flips through its pages.
"Evan Early sure has been in the hospital a long time," she says.

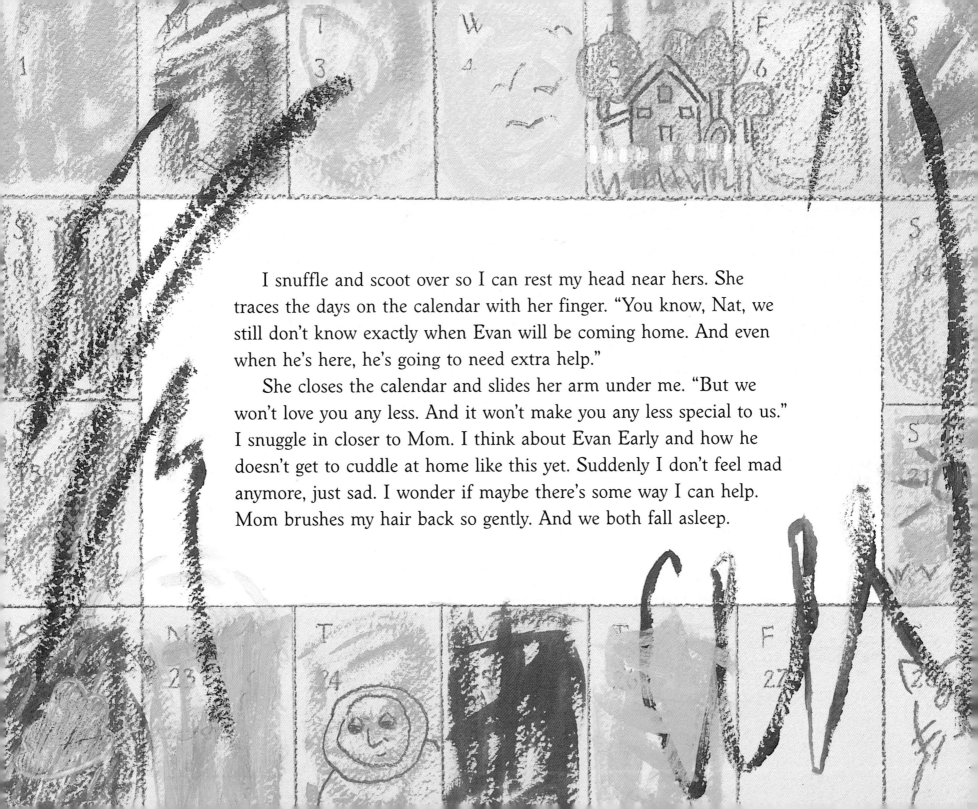

I snuffle and scoot over so I can rest my head near hers. She traces the days on the calendar with her finger. "You know, Nat, we still don't know exactly when Evan will be coming home. And even when he's here, he's going to need extra help."

She closes the calendar and slides her arm under me. "But we won't love you any less. And it won't make you any less special to us." I snuggle in closer to Mom. I think about Evan Early and how he doesn't get to cuddle at home like this yet. Suddenly I don't feel mad anymore, just sad. I wonder if maybe there's some way I can help. Mom brushes my hair back so gently. And we both fall asleep.

The next day, Mom takes me to visit Evan Early
and Dad. When we get there, I see that the machines are
back again, humming and snorting.

After hugging Dad, I stretch my hand out to touch Evan Early's tiny one. His
dandelion stem fingers curl around mine. It may still be a long time until he comes home, but I guess
I can start teaching him about our family here in the hospital.

I gently squeeze his hand twice.

"Love you, Evan Early."

Questions & Answers
about Prematurity

Question: Why are some babies born too early?

Most babies grow inside their mothers for nine months, allowing enough time to develop all the body parts they need to be healthy. Babies born before their nine months are up are called premature babies, or preemies. Sometimes babies are born early because they are sick or their mother is sick. Sometimes the mother's body has a hard time taking care of the baby, or the mother is carrying more than one baby inside her. We don't always know the reason why some babies are born early.

Question: Why does Evan look like a raw chicken? Will he always look like that?

When babies are born early, their skin is very thin and they don't yet have the layers of fat that other babies have. Because the skin is so thin, you can see the blood flowing beneath it. This makes it look reddish-purple. Some preemies have not yet grown their tougher top layer of skin, so their skin looks smooth and shiny. Evan's skin will grow thicker and start to look like a regular baby's as he grows older.

Question: Why does the nurse have to check Evan's diaper?

Nurses keep track of everything about premature babies, and they can tell a lot about how babies are doing by checking their diapers. Evan's nurse can tell how much food he is eating, how well his insides are working, if he's getting enough water, and if his medicines are helping him—all by looking in his diaper!

Question: Why do preemies sleep so much?

All new babies sleep a lot while their brains and bodies develop and grow. Preemies sleep even more because they have a lot of catching up to do. Some babies are born so early they can't yet open their eyes, and others might take medicine that makes them even sleepier. But all babies stay awake more as they grow older.

Question: Is Evan sick? Can Natalie catch it?

Evan's not exactly sick. His body just needs more time and help from the doctors and nurses to grow bigger and stronger. He may need medicine and surgery to make his body work the way it should. Natalie can't get sick from Evan, but she does need to make sure that she doesn't bring germs to Evan that can make him sick. Since Evan's body is so tiny and weak, even a cold can be very dangerous to him.

Question: What will Evan be like when he is older?

Many preemies end up just like any other kid, but some may always need a little extra time to learn and do things. Preemies are more likely to have problems with their eyes, their hearing, and their speech, but every baby is unique and grows up to have different strengths and needs.

Question: Why can't the doctors tell Evan's family when he will come home?

Some babies need more help than others, so it's very hard for doctors to say how long a baby's stay in the hospital might be. Evan's doctors will let him go home when he gets big enough, when he's gaining weight steadily, when he can keep his body temperature even, and when he can drink milk on his own. Most preemies stay in the hospital up until two to four weeks before the date they were supposed to be born.

Question: Why do Evan's parents have to spend so much time at the hospital?

Evan is getting lots of tests to see how his body is working. His parents want to be there so they know how he's doing and can get their questions answered. They are worried about him and want to help him feel safe and cared for, just like they would comfort Natalie if she were hurt or sick.

Question: Is Evan more special than his sister? Do his parents love him more?

No. All kids are special and all kids need love and attention. Evan's parents are just very worried about him and this sometimes makes them worn out. But they know Natalie is special in her own way and they love her just as much.